I didn't want to talk about it.

"Jodi?" asked Lauren in a hurt voice. "Is it true?"

"How come you didn't tell all of us?" demanded Cindi.

"I just found out for sure last night," I protested. "I didn't have time to tell you."

"You had time to pick fights with us," said Lauren. "You had time to tell us what's wrong with Patrick and with the rest of us, but you didn't have time to tell us this incredible news."

"Maybe it's not such incredible news to Jodi," said Darlene softly.

**Look for these and other books
in THE GYMNASTS series:**

THE GYMNASTS

#12 OUT OF CONTROL

Elizabeth Levy

AN
APPLE
PAPERBACK

SCHOLASTIC INC.
New York Toronto London Auckland Sydney

ISBN 0-590-42824-1

Copyright © 1990 by Elizabeth Levy. All rights reserved. Published by Scholastic Inc. APPLE PAPERBACKS is a registered trademark of Scholastic Inc. THE GYMNASTS is a trademark of Scholastic Inc.

12 11 10 9 8 7 6 5 4 3 2   0 1 2 3 4 5/9

Printed in the U.S.A.   28

First Scholastic printing, July 1990

To Murray—
for teaching me my own strengths
once again

There Ought to Be a Law

Almost every Tuesday morning, Mom wakes me up singing an old song. "They call it Stormy Monday, but Tuesday's just as bad . . ." Mom has a song for every day of the week, and she can't carry a tune. She's tone-deaf. She thinks it's funny. There ought to be a law against mothers singing in the morning. Sometimes I think the reason my dad and she got divorced is that Dad did not think Mom's singing was funny. In fact, Dad never loved rock and roll or rhythm and blues. His favorite music was country and western.

Barking Barney is the man that Mom is currently dating. He claims to love all different kinds of music. Isn't Barking Barney a ridiculous name for a grown man? I think so. He runs a chain of pet stores around Colorado, and each pet store is called Barking Barney's. Barking Barney is famous for his radio ads. Every week it's a different stupid riddle. This week it's, "Where did the three little kittens find their mittens?" The answer, in case you haven't heard it, is, "In the Yellow Pages."

As if Barking Barney weren't embarrassing enough, he's got a son. I call his son Nick the Pest. He's eight years old, and his dad thinks Nick is the smartest thing on two feet. Two left feet, maybe. Nick is clumsy. He's taking gymnastics just to be a copycat, but he's not very good. I think Nick's dumb. He believes calling me "Jodi-podi" is the height of originality. As far as I'm concerned, both Barking Barney and Nick the Pest could fall off the face of the earth and we'd all be better off.

Mom feels differently. Very differently.

"Wake me up before you go-go," I sang in a low growl to Mom from under my pillow.

Mom laughed. She turned the rod on my venetian blinds. "Jodi, it is really pouring out. Would I lie to you?"

"That's the title of another song," I groaned. Mornings aren't my best time. I looked out the window. The sky was dark gray, but I couldn't see the rain. We used to live in St. Louis, where there was a lot of rain, but it was never as depressing as a rainy day in Denver is. Maybe it's because we have fewer rainy mornings in the Rockies. It was spring, but spring here isn't half as nice as it used to be in St. Louis. It almost never starts until June, and then it gets hot quickly.

Mom pulled the pillow off my head. "Rise and shine, Jodi," she called.

I glared at her. Now I remembered that I wasn't just depressed about the rain. I was mad at her from the night before.

"Don't look at me that way," warned Mom.

"It's just my common-ordinary-everyday-walking around-normal-Tuesday-morning look," I lied.

Mom shrugged. I knew she didn't want to continue last night's discussion any more than I did. I got out of bed.

On the top of my dresser, LaToya swam up to the top of her little aquarium. LaToya is a frog. I got her as a tadpole a few months ago. She was a birthday present from Barney. She could win a stupid pet contest. She doesn't do anything except swim around a silly plastic flower.

"You're a stupid frog," I said to LaToya. The only good thing about LaToya is that I can say mean things to her and I don't think I hurt her feelings. She can't hear me.

I fed LaToya a few dried fish pellets. My bedroom is tiny, and most of it is filled with a low beam that I use to practice my gymnastics. When we had a big house back in St. Louis we kept the practice beam in the basement, but now Mom lets me keep it in my bedroom, which is usually full of dirty clothes. I pushed them aside and found something to wear that wasn't too filthy. Then I went downstairs for breakfast.

Mom made me oatmeal. It tasted better than LaToya's fish pellets. I tried one once. They taste very salty. Oatmeal's better, but it's not my favorite food in the world. Mom and I didn't talk much at breakfast.

"I'll see you at the gym this afternoon," said Mom. Mom is a gymnastics coach at the Evergreen Gymnastics Academy where I'm on a team called the Pinecones. Mom used to *own* a gymnastics school in St. Louis with my dad. Now, she just works for Patrick, my coach. She teaches the boys' team.

"Does Patrick know?" I asked Mom.

She sighed. "I'm going to tell him this afternoon. Jodi, it's not a secret. Some people would even think I have good news."

"Maybe Patrick will talk you out of it," I said. Now it was Mom's turn to glare at me. "Jodi, I don't *want* to be talked out of it. I'm very happy with my decision, and I know that in time you will be, too."

"Oh, sure," I said. "Are you going to tell me that you're doing this for me?"

"No," said Mom. "I'm doing it for me." Mom and I both have a temper. We try not to lose it at the same time, because when we do, boy, sparks fly. Mom took a deep breath. "Jodi, why don't you give yourself a few days to get used to the idea, and then we can talk about it more. I think it's perfectly normal to feel upset."

"Thanks. That makes me feel much better," I said sarcastically.

Mom sighed again. "Maybe you should talk about it with the Pinecones," she suggested. "They're your friends. They can help you sort things out."

I kind of grunted. There are six kids on my gymnastic team, and we are all pretty tight. I'd have to say that my teammates are my best friends, particularly the three that I started with: Darlene Broderick, Cindi Jockett, and Lauren Baca. We have two younger kids on our team: Ti An Troung, who I like, and Ashley Frank, who's a bit of a pill.

Darlene, Cindi, and Lauren are three of the best friends anybody could have. They're funny, loyal, and smart. The problem wasn't the Pinecones — it was Mom. I didn't want to talk to the Pinecones about my mom's decision.

I packed my knapsack with my schoolbooks and my gym bag with my shorts and T-shirt. Every afternoon, it was the same routine — a day at school and then two hours at the gym. No wonder I was in a bad mood. I never get to take a nap.

"Now what are you scowling about?" asked Mom. "Jodi, I already told you how sorry I am that you're upset."

"Look, Mom," I argued, "whatever you do is fine. It's your life. I think it's fine."

"You're still scowling," said Mom. I could tell that she was trying to be nice to me. All she wanted to do was tease me out of my bad mood, but I couldn't just change the way I felt to make her feel better.

"Did you ever think that I could be frowning and it doesn't have anything to do with you?" I yelled. I was dangerously close to getting really mad.

"Jodi, of course, I know your life doesn't revolve around me, but you've had some upsetting news."

"Well, that's not at all what I'm upset about. I'm upset about the fact that I never get to take a nap."

Mom stared at me. "You hate naps. As a little

kid I could never get you to take a nap. Jennifer always loved to take naps. She'd go to sleep as soon as I put her down, but you always had to be up and about." Jennifer is my older sister. She's eighteen, and Mom and Dad's divorce hasn't seemed to bother her much. Jennifer's nearly perfect. She's at the Air Force Academy and she's going to serve in the Air Force and then be a pilot or even an astronaut. Jennifer's got her whole life planned out. I can't even plan for next week.

"People change," I argued. "Maybe now that I'm eleven I need to nap. I never have time. I read in the paper that they have scientifically proved that people need naps."

Mom laughed. "You sound like your friend Lauren. Doesn't she say everything is a scientific fact?"

Lauren Baca is just about my very best friend on the gymnastics team. "You've got it *all* wrong," I told Mom. "Lauren says 'it's a proven fact,' not 'it's a scientific fact.' You just don't listen."

"Excuse me," she said, giving me a little bow. "I got one word wrong."

"It's not just a word — it's the whole way Lauren talks," I complained. "You just don't listen. You only hear what you want to hear."

Mom gave me the eye. It's the eye all mothers

give when they think they know the feelings underneath your words. I wonder if all moms get it wrong as much as my mom does. "I don't think we're arguing about Lauren's speech habits," she said.

"That just shows how little you know," I said. "That's exactly what this fight is about."

Mom just sighed again. There ought to be a law against sighing mothers. If this were a perfect world there would be. But it's not a perfect world. Mom just didn't realize it.

Where Does an 800-Pound Gorilla Sit?

I walked into the locker room. Lauren's gym bag was plunked down on the bench in front of my locker. I could tell it was Lauren's because it had teddy bear stickers all over it. Lauren has always loved teddy bears, particularly Terrence, the one she's had since she was a baby. She puts them everywhere, just the way she puts her gym bag everywhere.

"Will you get this out of the way?" I yelled. "Where am I supposed to put my stuff?" I waved my own gym bag in the air a little closer to Lauren's head than I should have.

Lauren ducked. "Sorry," she said. "It's a proven fact that you put your gym bag in front of my locker all the time."

"Jodi's gym bag always wanders," said Cindi.

Part of me knew that Cindi and Lauren were right. No one would ever accuse me of being a neatness freak. Still, Lauren had ticked me off.

"So where am I supposed to sit?" I demanded.

"Where *does* an 800-pound gorilla sit?" asked Darlene.

"Anywhere it wants?" said Ti An with a giggle. Ti An looked so pleased with herself. Ti An loves it when she gets a joke — that's because she doesn't get them a lot of the time.

"Are you all comparing me to a gorilla?" I asked.

Ti An is tiny. She's only nine, and she has very small bones. I kind of tower over her.

"Oh, no . . . of course not," Ti An stammered. I hadn't meant to scare her as much as I did.

Darlene giggled. "I just meant that in the mood you're in you're a little like an 800-pound gorilla."

"Thanks very much," I said, putting my hands on my hips.

Darlene put her arm around me. "Hey, Jodi, we're only kidding. Lighten up." She winked at me. Darlene and I are pretty close. I knew that some of the Pinecones are scared of my temper, but Darlene would never be scared of me. Darlene's tall. She's thirteen, the oldest of the Pinecones. She's the daughter of "Big Beef" Broderick, who plays football for the Denver Broncos.

Darlene is beautiful. I never had a black friend before Darlene. She loves new clothes. The saying "Born to Shop" was made for her. Today she was wearing an orange-and-yellow tie-dyed T-shirt over bicycle pants. I can't wear orange, but it looked great on Darlene. Darlene saw me staring at her T-shirt.

"Do you like it?" she asked.

I nodded. "Yeah, but . . ." I bit my tongue, literally. I knew that what I had been about to blurt out would really hurt Darlene. But I couldn't help wondering why she needed to have a new outfit *every day.*

"But what?" Darlene prompted.

"Nothing," I said, slipping on my old T-shirt, which was a hand-me-down from my sister.

Darlene looked at her watch. Even her Swatch watch matched her outfit. "We've got plenty of time. What were you going to say?"

I could feel myself blushing. Somehow Darlene knew that she wasn't going to like what was on my mind. She couldn't just leave it alone. It wasn't my fault that she was pushing me so hard.

"Okay," I said. "I don't know why you always have to show off how wealthy you are," I said.

Darlene's eyes widened and she got a funny look on her face.

"That's out of line," she said.

"Every day you come in with a new outfit," I said. "Well, some of us have to live with a clothes allowance."

"I know that," said Darlene.

"I know you do," I said. The truth is that Darlene is generous and kind, and I was the one who was being mean and spiteful.

"What's *really* bothering you today?" Darlene asked.

"Nothing," I groaned. "Just nothing." I felt bad. I knew that I had really hurt Darlene's feelings. "I'm sorry," I said. "Okay?"

"Okay," she said. Darlene isn't the type of kid to carry a grudge. It's not her fault that her dad earns so much money. Maybe if my dad had been a football player instead of a gymnast, I'd be into clothes, too. Nobody ever goes into gymnastics for the money, that's what Dad says. I wonder if Dad had made a lot of money whether it would have made a difference to Mom. I'll never know the answer to that question.

I sighed.

"What's with the sighs and groans?" asked Cindi.

"I am not sighing and groaning," I protested.

"You sure are doing a good imitation," said Lauren.

"Why don't you all just shut up?" I cried, and I ran out of the locker room. I could see that the Pinecones were all shocked. I was sick of people asking me how I felt. I knew how I felt. I felt like a worm, and all I wanted to do was to eat dirt. It's not exactly the right mood to go out on the gym floor and practice gymnastics. In fact, it's the kind of mood that can get you hurt.

3

Off With Her Head

Inside the gym, I could see Mom working with the boys' team. She was spotting Jared, Cindi's brother, on the rings. Mom has a look of total concentration when she's teaching gymnastics. She didn't even notice me as I walked to the end of the gym where Patrick was waiting for us.

"What's wrong with Jodi?" I heard Cindi whisper in back of me.

"Leave her alone," whispered Darlene. "She's just in a bad mood. She'll snap out of it."

"I *am not* in a bad mood," I said, turning around so quickly I half twisted my ankle.

" 'Off with her head' said the Queen," said Lauren.

"And what does that mean?" I asked, rubbing

my ankle. I was exaggerating how much it hurt. It didn't, but I guess I wanted the Pinecones to feel sorry for me.

"We've been studying *Alice in Wonderland* in school," said Lauren. "You sound just like the crazy queen who keeps yelling 'Off with her head!' during a miniature golf tournament."

"It's a croquet game," I said. "Just because you're in the talented and gifted program, you don't know everything. My father read me *Alice in Wonderland* when I was just a little kid."

"I was making a joke," said Lauren.

"Well, I am not a crazy queen!" I shouted.

Lauren giggled nervously.

Just then Becky Dyson walked by. Becky hates me, but that's okay. She hates all the Pinecones. Being hated by Becky is almost a compliment. Dad always says that talent has nothing to do with personality. He's taught a lot of elite gymnasts, and he always told me never to mistake personality for talent. "Some of the great gymnasts are also great people, but some of them are real stinkers."

Becky is definitely in the real stinker category. Unfortunately, she's also one of the most talented gymnasts I've ever seen. Fortunately, she's too good to be a Pinecone. She's in Patrick's advanced group, the Needles. The Pinecones are still intermediates.

Becky is blonde like me, and she's got the perfect gymnast's body. She's long-waisted with short legs. She's steady as a rock on the balance beam, which is probably her best event. Actually her very best event is making trouble for the Pinecones.

Becky gave me one of her patented put-down stares. "Jodi Sutton, you couldn't be queen of anything."

"Don't worry, Becky," said Cindi. "You are the all-time record-holding queen."

"Thank you," said Becky, not realizing that Cindi had intended it as an insult.

Cindi started laughing uncontrollably. When Cindi gets going, she snorts and stamps her left foot.

"What's so funny?" Becky asked. "I'd make a better queen than Jodi, any day."

Cindi was laughing so hard she couldn't answer.

Patrick came up. He was smiling. Patrick is pretty young to be running his own gym, and he jokes around with us a lot. He was a top-rated college gymnast. "Would anyone mind sharing the joke with me?" he asked.

"Becky and Jodi are arguing about who should be crowned Crazy Queen," said Lauren.

"I was not arguing," I objected.

Becky looked thoroughly confused. Patrick burst out laughing. "I've heard a lot of silly arguments in my gym," he said, "but this one takes the cake."

Becky didn't seem to think that Patrick was funny. "It's typical Pinecone humor," she said.

"Then, Becky, I think you'd better go warm up with your own group," said Patrick. "Besides, the Pinecones and I have our work cut out for us today."

Becky walked away with her toes turned out. She'll tell you that she walks that way because of all her dance training, but honestly, it just makes her look stuck-up.

Darlene grabbed my hand and waved it over our heads. "Let's declare Jodi Queen for the Day," she announced. I knew Darlene was trying to jolly me out of my bad mood. Nobody would ever try to jolly Becky out of one of her snits. It wasn't worth it. I tried to grin at Darlene.

"Okay, my Pinecone Queen, let's see how you do on the uneven bars today," said Patrick.

"Don't call me queen," I snapped without thinking what I was saying. Patrick stared at me.

"Sorry," I muttered. I tried to make a joke. "Becky made it clear that she's the only queen around here."

Patrick adjusted the uneven bars for me. "You

like them almost at the max, don't you?" he asked, moving the bars nearly one-and-a-half feet apart.

I was putting the chalk on my hands. "Don't you have it written down?" I asked Patrick. "My dad used to write down to the caliber of a hundredth of an inch exactly what each gymnast needed on the uneven bars, and he did it for the vault, too."

Patrick gave me a funny look.

"What?" I asked. "I'm just giving you a helpful hint," I said.

"Jodi, I've been coaching you for a long time, and you haven't needed to give me helpful hints before. I'm the coach here, remember?"

I clapped my hands together to get off the loose chalk.

I kicked up and over the lower bar. "Okay, do a skin-the-cat to a stride support," said Patrick.

"That's a move for babies," I argued. "Skin-the-cat is something every little kid does on a jungle gym."

"It's a good way to get from the upper to the lower bar. Just tuck your legs through your arms while hanging upside down. I've got some ideas that I'm working out for your new routine, but first I want you to be solid on your fundamentals."

"I would think by this time that I'd be way

beyond fundamentals," I muttered under my breath.

"I'm going to pretend I didn't hear that," said Patrick. "Nobody here is beyond fundamentals. They're our building blocks."

"Baby blocks," I said under my breath. I knew I should keep my mouth shut, but I just couldn't.

I sat on the lower bar and reached out with my hands for the upper bars. Then I swung down and pulled my legs up.

"No, no, Jodi," said Patrick. "Use the rebound of the lower bar. Put a little more oomph into your swing. But it needs to be controlled oomph."

" 'Controlled oomph' is not a gymnastics term," I argued. "I don't understand what it means."

"Well, think about it." Patrick grinned at me. "Controlled oomph."

"It sounds like two things that don't go together. It sounds stupid," I said.

"Oomph means put a little more energy into your gymnastics and a little less into your back talk," he said. "That goes for all the Pinecones." I could feel myself blushing. Normally, we get along just great. My teachers at school hate my back talk, but I could never remember Patrick chiding me for it. I must have hit a nerve with him.

I finished my routine and swung down from the bars. Patrick called Ti An.

I sat back down on the mats between Darlene and Cindi. "Hey, kiddo," said Darlene. "Cool it with Patrick. It takes a lot to get him annoyed. What *is* wrong with you today?"

My teammates were driving me a little crazy. "Did it ever occur to you that *nothing* might be wrong with me? Maybe I have a legitimate complaint."

"Come on," joked Cindi. "Complaining that Patrick used the word 'oomph.' You think that's a legitimate complaint?"

"It just so happens that my father is one of the best gymnastics coaches in the country, and he would never say something like 'put a little oomph into your swing.' That's stupid."

"Are you calling Patrick stupid?" Cindi demanded.

"No, of course not," I said, glancing at Patrick who was spotting Ti An. I'm sure he thought that Ti An had plenty of oomph. Patrick said something that set Ti An giggling.

There isn't much giggling in my dad's gym. Maybe giggling wasn't always a good thing. Dad always said there was such a thing as too much laughing in a gym. A gym should be a place of serious learning. Maybe he was right.

4

Stupid on the Brain

It was the first time in a long time that I was really glad when practice was over. I wished I could wave a magic wand and make my mood go away, but it stuck around, making the skin around my eyes feel all scratchy. Part of me was scared that maybe if I stayed in a mood like this I'd actually turn into Becky.

In fairy tales, bad thoughts have power. If that was true, I had enough bad thoughts to light up Denver.

Mom put the boys' team through their cool-downs. Mom was joking with Cindi's brother Jared. Jared was grinning. He said something, and Mom started laughing so hard it was a little bit embarrassing. Mom has a snort that she makes when she's laughing too hard. It's a little like Cindi's laugh. It's really pretty disgusting.

"Say, Jodi, aren't you coming to change?" Cindi asked me, startling me. I hoped she wasn't able to read my mind. "What's so fascinating over at the boys' team?"

"Maybe Jodi's in love," teased Lauren. "Maybe that's why she's in a bad mood."

"Being in love is supposed to put you in a good mood," protested Darlene. "I don't think Jodi's in love."

"Maybe she's in love with someone who doesn't love her," said Ashley giggling.

"I'm not," I snapped. "Believe me, that's the least of my worries."

"Besides, eleven-year-olds aren't supposed to be in love," said Ashley. Ashley always sounds so prissy. "Patrick wouldn't like it."

"Who cares what Patrick likes?" I muttered.

"Well, speaking as a Pinecone, I can't wait for tomorrow," said Lauren.

"Why?" I asked.

"Because you obviously got up on the wrong side of the bed today. It's a proven fact that rarely does a person get up on the wrong side of the bed two days in a row."

"Very funny," I said.

Just then Jared came up to us. He had

wrapped a towel around his neck. I think Jared has a little bit of a crush on Darlene, and I expected that Darlene was the one he wanted to talk to. I started to walk away.

"Hey, Jodi!" yelled Jared.

I turned around. "What?" I asked.

"I just wanted to congratulate you," said Jared.

"On what?" asked Lauren. "What did Jodi do?"

"It's nothing," I muttered. I didn't want anybody's congratulations. As far as I was concerned, there was absolutely nothing to be congratulated about.

"Hey, Jodi, way to go," said Ryan, Jared's best friend. "Marrying into a pet store dynasty! That's terrific."

Lauren's, Cindi's, and Darlene's mouths fell open in unison. If they hadn't looked so shocked, it might have been funny. I always thought that mouths dropping open in surprise was just a phrase, but when I watched my three best friends, I knew it was true.

"What?" exclaimed Cindi. "What are you guys talking about?"

"Didn't Jodi tell you that her mom's getting married to Barking Barney?" said Ryan.

"Jodi?" asked Lauren, in a hurt voice. "Is it true?"

I licked my tongue around the edges of my lips.

My mouth felt incredibly dry. I looked down at the lines on the gym floor. I wanted to look anywhere except at the faces of my friends.

"I don't know why Mom had to blabber the news to all the boys," I said.

"Well, she said she'll be taking a two-week honeymoon in a while because she was getting married, and she didn't want us to hear about it from anyone else," said Jared. "I guess she figured Cindi would tell me. Now that I think about it, Cindi, I'm pretty p.o.'d that *you* didn't tell me."

"I didn't know!" said Cindi furiously. She glared at me.

"You're kidding," crowed Jared. "You mean I knew something before you did! How come Jodi didn't tell you?"

"I don't know," said Cindi through gritted teeth. "Jodi how come you didn't tell me?"

"How come you didn't tell all of us?" demanded Lauren. "I can't believe you let the boys find out about this before the Pinecones did."

"I just found out for sure last night," I protested. "I didn't have time to tell you."

"You had time to pick fights with us," said Lauren. "You had time to tell us what's wrong with Patrick and with the rest of us, but you didn't have time to tell us this incredible news."

"Maybe it's not such incredible news to Jodi," said Darlene softly.

I looked at her, glad that at least one person understood.

I hated the fact that Mom was getting remarried. I didn't want Nick the Pest for a brother. I didn't want someone with a stupid name like Barking Barney to be my so-called stepfather.

I felt guilty. Feeling guilty always makes me mad. I turned and ran toward the locker room, but not fast enough — Patrick was in my way.

"Jodi, congratulations," he said.

"I didn't do anything," I complained. Why did everyone think that I deserved congratulations just because my mother was getting married? If it were my choice, it wouldn't be happening at all.

"I meant on your mom getting married. I think it's wonderful. I'm happy for all of you," said Patrick.

I forced myself to take a deep breath. "Thanks," I managed to mutter. "I've got to go." I fled into the locker room. I tried to open my locker door. It was stuck. I pulled the handle. I shook it so hard that the entire row of lockers almost toppled down on me.

"Trying to tear the place down?" asked Darlene. She and the rest of the Pinecones had followed me into the locker room.

"The stupid thing is stuck. Nothing works the way it's supposed to in here," I grumbled.

"You know, I think that sometimes," said Ashley. "I keep thinking how nice the Atomic Amazons' locker room was."

"Ashley, shut up," said Lauren.

"No," I argued. "Ashley's got a point. I know that Patrick doesn't have much money to fix this place up, but he could at least have lockers that open and close."

I got my stuff out of my locker and slammed the door, but the locker door really didn't close right. I had to jiggle the bottom to make it close.

"Will you shut up about lockers?" exclaimed Lauren. "Tell us about your mom getting married. I can't believe we had to find out from somebody else."

"I just found out myself," I said. "And I didn't think it was anybody else's business."

"Business?" exclaimed Cindi. "Who's talking about business? I think it's so romantic. What are you going to wear?"

"An Evergreen leotard," I said sarcastically.

"You know, it could be pretty with a green skirt," said Darlene. "Is that really what your mom wants you to wear?"

I picked up my gym bag and sighed. "Believe me, I don't know *or* care what I'm wearing to this stupid wedding. I've got other things on my mind."

"Yeah, like complaining about the lockers,"

said Lauren. She sat down on the bench right in front of my locker. "Come off it, Jodi. You've got to be excited. Just imagine the pets you're going to get. I wonder if Barking Barney will give you an expensive Siamese cat as a present."

"I don't want a cat. I don't even like having to take care of my tadpole."

"LaToya's a frog now," said Lauren. "I think she's cute."

"Great, I'll let you clean her aquarium every week. She stinks up my whole room."

"I thought it was sweet the way LaToya came in the mail in a little carton that looked like Chinese food," said Lauren.

"It was a stupid, babyish present. I'm not a baby. And now I have to take care of the stupid thing."

"I think Jodi's got stupid on her brain," said Darlene.

"Thank you very much," I said. "With that compliment, I hope you'll all excuse me."

Darlene put her hand on my arm. "Jodi, wait. We're sorry we teased you. Don't you want to talk about your mom getting married?"

"No, I do not," I said. "It's got nothing to do with me or you."

"Nothing to do with you?" said Cindi. "It'll change everything for you. If it were happening to me, I'd want to talk about it with my friends."

"Well, it's not happening to you, is it?" I said sarcastically. Cindi comes from one of those picture-perfect families that look like they belong on television. Her parents have never been divorced. She's got four older brothers and she lives in a big house. Her parents have been married forever and probably have never had an argument in their lives. In fact, I had never realized it before, but *none* of the Pinecones could understand what I was going through. All of them came from happy families. Darlene and her family were always appearing in magazines because they were so photogenic. Lauren was an only child, but her parents had never been divorced. Everybody else had been born in Denver. No wonder they felt so at home at a place called the Evergreen Gymnastics Academy. I wasn't born in the Rockies. I was born in the Midwest. I wasn't a Denver Bronco fan. I rooted for my baseball team, the St. Louis Cardinals.

All the other Pinecones did gymnastics just because they thought it was fun. Both my mom and dad had been champions. My sister was a champion. Everybody thought it was so sweet that Patrick didn't push me. Maybe the reason that he didn't was because he was satisfied with the Pinecones just being mediocre. My dad would never tolerate a mediocre team. Just thinking about the fact that Patrick didn't push us made me mad.

"Earth to Jodi . . . Earth to Jodi . . ." said Lauren. "We were talking about your mom's wedding. Where did you go?"

"I've got more important things to think about," I said.

"What could be more important than your mom's wedding?" Cindi asked.

"There!" I said. "That's exactly what's wrong with the Pinecones."

The Pinecones all stared at each other as if I had stopped making sense. But I knew exactly what I meant.

5

Don't Bop the Coach
on the Nose

I refused to get involved in Mom's plans for the wedding. I told her that whatever she did was fine. I think she was a little bit hurt, but I had other things on my mind.

All week nothing really went right at the gym. Patrick wanted us to work on our floor routines, particularly our dance moves. I find dance moves boring. I'd much rather be learning complicated new tricks.

Instead, Patrick was taking us back to basics.

"Jodi, round your arms," Patrick said. "Remember your wrists and hands are supposed to be an extension of the curve made by your arms. They're not just supposed to flop. Control is the key, here."

"I don't care what I look like dancing. I need to get on to do some more difficult tricks for my floor routine," I complained.

"Jodi, you're the one who needs the most work on your dance routine."

"I do?" I asked defiantly. I put my hands on my hips, something that I knew I had been doing a lot of lately. "I don't think the judges care about my dance. I need to work on my back flips."

"Jodi, I'm the coach. I'll be the judge of what you need to work on." Patrick's voice was soft, but I knew that he wasn't amused. We hadn't been getting along well this week. All he could talk about was fundamentals, but I wasn't in the mood for fundamentals.

Finally Patrick clapped his hands together, a signal that we were moving on to a new skill.

"Since Jodi wants to practice back flips, that's what we'll do," he said.

"All right!" said Darlene, stretching out her hand for me to slap. "I love back flips, too."

I gave her hand a slap, but it was a halfhearted high-five. Even though I was getting my own way, I still didn't feel very good about it.

"Okay, Jodi, you first," said Patrick.

I stepped onto the mats. "I'll do it from a roundoff," I said.

Patrick shook his head. "No, I want you to work from a standing position."

"But that's so boring," I argued. "And it looks ugly."

Patrick gave me a patient stare over the top of his clipboard.

"Fundamentals," I groaned.

He nodded.

It's very hard to do a back flip without a run for momentum, but it *is* the way that Patrick had taught us. My dad always taught kids to do it from a roundoff. A roundoff to back flip gives you much more punch.

I put my hands over my head.

"Remember, think sitting in a chair before anything else," said Patrick.

I lowered my hands and crouched down. Dad always says that it's not natural to jump backward, and so it's better to just run and do it without thinking. Sometimes I think Patrick makes us think too much.

I sprang up and arched my back to flip over into a handstand, but I didn't have enough momentum and my hands buckled under me. I ended up on my knees.

"More control, Jodi," said Patrick. "Spot your hands as you go into the flip. Keep your eyes on your hands as they are about to touch the mat."

"It would be easier if I could have a running start," I said, rolling over on my side. I rubbed my elbow.

"Did you hurt yourself?" Patrick asked.

I shook my head.

"Good," he said. "Try it again."

"What about the rest of us?" whined Ashley. "How come Jodi's getting all this special attention?"

"You'll get your turn," said Patrick. "I just want to get Jodi under control."

"That's not a bad idea," teased Darlene. "It'll help the rest of us."

"Yeah," said Cindi. "We could use a control button on Jodi these days."

"That's not funny!" I snapped. I was in a lousy mood.

Patrick gave me a smile. I never noticed it before, but Patrick smiles an awful lot, almost too much.

"Okay, Jodi, try it again," he said.

"I'll never do a good back flip unless you let me take a running start," I complained.

"It'll work if you would just concentrate," said Patrick. "I'm right here to spot you."

He stood behind me with his arms out. "I don't need a spot to do just a stupid back flip," I told him. "Have you forgotten that I was practically born doing back flips? I'll bet my father was doing back flips before you were even born."

"Maybe," said Patrick. "But I'm not worried about your dad. I'm worried about you. Come on, Jodi. Let's have less talking and more gymnastics."

"Well, excuse me," I said sarcastically. I read in a magazine that sarcasm is a sign that a person is weak — that strong people aren't sarcastic. Becky Dyson is the strongest girl I know, and she's sarcastic all the time — so I don't see how it can be true.

Patrick put his hands on his hips. "Jodi, if you're not ready to work at gymnastics, I'll work with somebody else."

"I'm ready," I said. I tried to do the back flip again from a standing position. I leaned too far back and Patrick had to lift me around. I flung my arm wide to keep my balance. I slapped Patrick on the nose. Hard.

Patrick flipped me over to a standing position and rubbed his nose.

"Sorry," I said.

"It's okay," said Patrick. "It was an accident. You didn't mean it."

He waved to Ashley that she was next. I went back to stand with the Pinecones.

"You really bopped Patrick one," said Lauren with a giggle. "His nose is still red."

"I didn't mean to," I said. "My arms were just out of control. It's kind of his fault, because if I had been able to do it from a running position,

I would have been fine. I wouldn't have even needed a spot."

"You sure have an opinion about everything these days," said Darlene. "Why can't you just let Patrick be the coach?"

"I have a right to my opinions," I said. "It's a free country, or haven't you noticed?"

"I've noticed," said Darlene.

"Are you being sarcastic?" I challenged her.

"Me?" exclaimed Darlene. "You're the one who's got sarcasm on the brain, and I wish it would go away."

I watched Patrick work with Ashley. She did the standing back flip perfectly. While Patrick was talking to her, he absentmindedly rubbed his nose where I had hit him.

It *had* been an accident. I hadn't meant to hurt him, but when my arm flung out and I could sense how close Patrick was, I didn't pull my arm back. It was as if I couldn't. It was as if my arm wasn't in my control, and I wanted to hit something. Patrick's nose just happened to get in the way. But even *I* knew that it wasn't a good idea for a gymnast to go around bopping her coach on the nose. Even Patrick wouldn't let me get away with that forever.

6

Right Side or Wrong Side

Saturday I could finally sleep late. We didn't have a meet, and we didn't have practice. I had specifically asked Mom not to wake me up with a musical number. I had a day with no plans, just a little homework. Mom didn't know I was awake yet. It was eleven o'clock in the morning, and I had been lying in bed for an hour, but I didn't want to get up. It was totally private time, and I didn't want to talk to Mom. All she could talk about these days were plans for the wedding.

I heard the doorbell ring. Now I was so glad that I had stayed in bed. Mom had said Barney and his son were coming over for Saturday brunch. Mom had also said that Barney and Nick had a surprise for me.

The best surprise would be that Barney and Mom had decided to call off the wedding. The second best surprise would be to find out that Nick the Pest was being sent off to military school.

I watched LaToya swim to the top of her aquarium. The aquarium was getting cloudy, and I knew I'd have to change her water today. LaToya had an easy life — no mother announcing that she was marrying a new frog.

"I wish you would marry Barney," I whispered to LaToya. "Then you, Barney, and Nick the Pest could disappear into a magic bubble and I'd never see any of you again."

LaToya blew a bubble at me. I laughed.

Suddenly I heard someone whispering outside my door. Quickly I jumped back in bed. It had to be Nick the Pest wanting to play. I would pretend I was asleep, and maybe he would go away.

I peeked out from under my pillow and watched my door. The knob began to turn.

The nerve of that twerp! How dare he just walk in my room without knocking. This was really going too far. I'd teach him a lesson!

I grabbed my pillow. As the door opened a crack, I heaved the pillow with all my might. It hit the door hard enough to swing it shut, but the latch didn't catch. I'm pretty strong, and I've got a good arm.

"Come one step further and it won't just be a pillow I hit you with," I warned as I saw the door opening again.

Darlene's head appeared below the doorknob. She had dropped down on all fours. "Duck, guys, it's a war zone in here," she said.

"Darlene!" I exclaimed.

Darlene sat back on her heels and started laughing.

"What are you doing here?" I asked.

I saw another face peering around the door. Ti An was looking in. "Is it safe?" she asked.

Behind Ti An stood Cindi and Lauren, and way behind Lauren, Ashley was holding back, standing very close to the wall.

"What are you *all* doing here?" I asked, jumping out of bed. I scratched my head. I was pretty sure that we hadn't made any plans to get together that I had forgotten about.

"This is a Pinecone mercy mission," said Darlene, shoving some of my clothes off the beam and sitting down. The other Pinecones followed her lead and they all perched on the beam, like a bunch of little birds. They stared at me.

"What are you staring at?" I asked.

"Get back into bed," said Darlene. "We have to check something."

"What?" I asked.

"Just do as we say," said Darlene. I climbed back onto my mattress. I giggled a little nervously. There was something very strange, and almost a little scary, about all the Pinecones appearing at my house on a Saturday morning after the awful way I had been acting lately. Darlene was smiling as if to reassure me that nobody was mad at me.

"I think she should get under the covers," said Cindi. "So that we make sure everything is done just right."

"Tell me what this is about," I begged. "Did Mom call you up and make you come over here?"

"No more questions," ordered Darlene. "Get under the covers."

I pushed my feet between the sheets and pulled the blanket over my head.

"Okay, good," said Darlene. "Now get out of bed naturally."

"Huh?" I really couldn't figure out what was going on.

"Just do as we say," said Darlene.

"Pretend we're not here," said Cindi.

"Is this a practical joke?" I asked. "Are you going to throw tadpoles at me or something if I get out of bed?"

"This is very serious scientific research," said Lauren. The others all nodded.

I couldn't imagine what was going on, but I did what I was told. I pushed the covers back and got out of bed.

I stood up in front of the Pinecones and raised my hands over my head as if I had just done a complicated vault and stuck my landing.

Darlene gestured for the other Pinecones to join her in a conference. "What do you think?" I heard her ask.

"I think it was nearly a perfect ten," said Cindi.

"And definitely on the right side," said Lauren. "It's a proven fact that she got up on the right side."

Ti An started laughing.

"Would you all mind letting me in on the big joke?" I asked.

"You've been in such a bad mood for the past couple of weeks that we decided we had to come over here this Saturday and *make sure* that you got out of bed on the *right* side."

I laughed, but a little uncomfortably. "Have I really been that bad?" I asked.

"Really," said Darlene.

The other Pinecones all nodded. "I guess I have been a stinker lately," I said. I expected them to disagree with me, but nobody did.

"Sorry," I said with a smile. It really meant a lot to me that they liked me even when I acted like a brat.

"Now that we know she got out of bed on the right side, let's go down and talk to Jodi's mom about the wedding," said Cindi excitedly.

The smile left my face. Darlene saw it. I could see her kind of gesture to Cindi to drop the subject. Suddenly it didn't seem so funny to me that the Pinecones had all made such a big deal about coming over on a Saturday morning. I didn't think their little joke about watching me get up on the *right* side of the bed was funny at all.

7

Loosey-Goosey

"What's the verdict?" Mom shouted up the stairs.

"Was Mom in on the joke?" I asked Darlene.

"She thought it was a good idea. She told us to tiptoe up here," said Darlene.

"It's okay, Ms. Sutton," yelled Cindi. "Jodi positively, absolutely got up on the right side of the bed."

"Then why don't you all come down and I'll make scrambled eggs," said Mom.

The Pinecones tumbled out of my room very quickly, as if scrambled eggs were the taste treat of the century. I got the feeling that they'd rather be with my mom than with me.

Darlene stuck around while I got dressed. I pulled on a pair of black jeans.

I looked down and noticed that my black jeans had smudges on them, but I didn't care. I glanced over at Darlene. She had a serious expression on her face. Darlene cares so much about clothes.

I pulled on a brown sweatshirt. Darlene gave me a funny look.

"*Now* what's wrong?" I demanded.

"I haven't said a word," she said.

"You're looking at me funny. What's wrong with what I'm wearing? It's my own house, for goodness' sake. I can wear what I want to in my own house."

"I just think that black and brown is a depressing combination. Can't you at least put on a white sweatshirt? Black and white looks much prettier."

"I don't have to look pretty in my own house," I said, grabbing a brush and giving it one pull through my messy hair. I put the brush down and glared defiantly at Darlene.

Darlene shrugged. "It's just that you're so pretty. You don't always have to be messy."

"Looking pretty isn't the only thing I care about," I said with just a tinge of sarcasm in my voice.

Darlene looked hurt.

"Jodi, Darlene . . . come on down quickly. Your eggs are getting cold," Mom yelled.

"I *hate* cold eggs," said Darlene. She emphasized the word "hate."

We went downstairs. Mom was sitting between Cindi and Lauren. Ti An was leaning over the table across from her. They were all grinning and laughing. Mom was in the middle of a sentence. She stopped when she saw me.

"Go on," I said.

"I'll get your eggs," said Mom.

"I can get them myself," I said. "What were you all laughing about?"

"Your mom was telling us about plans for the wedding," Ti An said.

"I'm sending out the invitations this week," said Mom. "All the Pinecones will be invited."

"Yippee!" exclaimed Cindi. "I love weddings. I was worried that it was going to be a small wedding and we wouldn't get to come."

"Well, originally Barney and I planned on a small wedding. It's a second wedding for both of us, and at first I didn't want to make a big deal out of it."

I muttered under my breath, as I took a bite of my scrambled eggs. They had gotten cold.

"Is anything wrong?" Mom asked.

"It's just that my eggs are cold," I said.

"I can put them in the microwave," said Mom. She started to take my plate. I grabbed it back. "It's okay. I like cold eggs," I said sarcastically. "Go on telling them about your plans. I'll bet they find it as ridiculous as I do."

"What's ridiculous about a wedding?" asked Darlene. "Weddings are beautiful."

"Wait till you hear what Mom's cooked up," I said. Mom had told me about her final plans for the wedding, but I hadn't told them to anybody in the hopes that she'd finally see what a fool she was making of herself. Now the invitations had been printed up and there was no turning back. I sat back in my chair. At least now Mom would hear from somebody like Darlene that her plan was in definite bad taste.

"Where's the wedding going to be?" Lauren asked.

"In the gym," said Mom. At least she had the decency to blush.

"Our gym!" shouted Ti An.

"Patrick offered to let us use the gym for the wedding. Barney and I realized that there were so many people that we really cared about, we needed a big place."

"Patrick's gym is a dump!" I said.

"It'll look beautiful with flowers," said Darlene. "We can all help decorate."

"It'll still look like a dump," I said. "What are you going to do, Mom, do back flips down the aisle?"

"Well, maybe that's not a bad idea," said Mom. She was laughing. "My first wedding was so stuffy. I like the idea of this wedding being looser."

"Jodi can do a flip from a standing position if she ever gets her arms under control," said Ti An.

"Yeah," said Lauren. "We wouldn't want Jodi bopping her new father in the nose, the way she did with Patrick."

"What's this about Jodi hitting Patrick on the nose?" Mom asked.

"It was an accident," I protested. "And besides, Lauren, Barney is *not* going to be my father."

Lauren looked embarrassed. I guess I had spoken louder than I realized.

Mom tried to change the subject. "Well, I'd still like a loosey-goosey wedding," she said.

I didn't tell her my wish. I didn't want any wedding at all.

8

Anteaters and Whiskers

The doorbell rang again. This time I knew who it was. Nick and Barney. Soon we'd all be living together. The thought of Nick coming into my house whenever he wanted to just made me sick. We were going to move soon after the wedding. Mom and Barney had found a house, not far from my own neighborhood, big enough for us all to live in. It had a new family room, because we would be a new family, and it had space in the basement for all our gym equipment. My bedroom would be bigger, and it was a real house, not a town house, with a big backyard, but I wasn't thrilled about moving. The new house also had a bedroom for Nick.

Luckily Nick lives with his own mother during the week, so Mom kept telling me that I'd have a little brother only on weekends. Personally I'd rather not have a little brother at all.

I could hear Mom laughing out in the vestibule.

"Your mom sounds so happy," said Cindi. "It's so neat that we're all being invited to the wedding, and that it's going to be in the gym."

"I'll have to decide what to wear," said Darlene. "I wonder what your bridesmaid's dress is going to look like."

"I hope it's black," I said. "That's the color that I told Mom I want."

"Black would be too old for you," said Darlene. "And I don't think it would be right for a wedding."

"A lot you know about taste," I said. "You think having a wedding in the gym is cool."

Before Darlene could answer me, Barking Barney burst into the room. Barney never does anything slowly. He's a little bit pudgy, and you'd think he'd move slowly, but he always looks like he's in a hurry.

"Uh-oh, Nick, it's a Pinecone convention," joked Barney. He had his arm around Mom's shoulders. "Sarah, you should have warned me that Jodi had company. I would have let Nick bring a couple more Amazons to protect us."

"Hi, Mr. Josephson," said Darlene and Lauren simultaneously.

Nick was carrying something behind his back, probably a water bomb — that's the kind of joke that Nick loves. He's always trying to play tricks on me. Luckily he's too little to think of good ones, and I can usually outsmart him.

He's got dark curly hair, and he's a teeny bit pudgy himself. He was wearing a red Atomic Amazons sweatshirt.

Barney gave me a kiss on a cheek. "How's my favorite bridesmaid doing?" he asked.

"Fine," I said. I caught Darlene watching me as if she didn't quite trust me to behave myself. I decided to try to be super-polite.

"How are you doing, Nick?" I asked.

Nick is used to me either ignoring him or growling at him. He shifted his feet a little nervously, but he didn't take his arms out from around his back.

"What do you have there, Nick?" I asked him.

"It's a present for you, Jodi," said Barney with a big smile.

My heart sank. The last present from Nick and Barney had been LaToya. All I needed right now was another animal to take care of.

"It's not Jodi's birthday," said Mom.

"This is just a present to welcome her into her new family," said Barney. Barney winked at Nick, who looked about as uncomfortable as I did.

I held out my hands to take the present.

"Not so fast," said Nick. "She's got to answer the riddle."

"Oh, goody," said Ti An. "This is just like one of your ads, Mr. Josephson."

"Barney," said Barney.

"Barney," repeated Ti An.

I was getting impatient. I kind of wanted to see what my present was. Maybe it was a baby python, and I could use it to strangle Nick. "What's my riddle?" I asked.

"What baby is born with whiskers?" Nick asked.

"An anteater," I said.

"That's wrong," said Nick.

"No it's not," I argued. "I bet you anything that an anteater is born with whiskers. I've got a picture of one somewhere in a book."

"Jodi's right," said Lauren. "It's a proven fact that an anteater is born with whiskers."

"Well, it's the wrong answer, isn't it, Dad?" said Nick with a pout.

Barney rubbed his chin. "Well, now, Jodi . . . it's the right answer, but think of something else that's born with whiskers."

"A lion," I said. "Lion cubs have long whiskers."

"At least you're in the right family," said Barney. "Keep going."

"Riddles shouldn't have more than one answer," I said. "Then it's not a good riddle."

"Jodi-podi got the wrong answer, and my arms are getting tired."

"I'll bet you've got an anteater behind your back, don't you?" I teased him.

"You're the ant," said Nick.

"Children," said Barney. "This is a happy time. Let's throw the riddle open to all the Pinecones. What baby is born with whiskers, girls?"

"A kitten!" exclaimed Ti An. "You've been running kitten ads for the past couple weeks."

I glared at her. It was such a weak answer.

"Very good," said Barney. "You've proved somebody's listening. Nick, give Jodi her present."

Nick handed me a white plastic cage about the size of two shoeboxes. The cage had wire mesh in the front and holes in the top. It was so light that it felt empty.

Mom was grinning at me. "I . . . I . . . " I was about to say that I didn't want a kitten, but Mom looked so hopeful that I would finally like something that Barney gave me that I didn't know what to say. I don't like cats. My dad is allergic, and we never had them when I was growing up. I'm a little afraid of cats. If Barking Barney wanted to give me a pet, he should have at least let me pick it out myself.

"Aren't you going to look at it?" asked Lauren, jumping up and peering over my shoulder.

I opened the cage door. I could hear something mewing softly.

"Here," said Nick. "You don't know how to pick up cats." He reached inside the cage and pulled out a little tiger kitten. It was orange, with kind of squiggly black lines all over its body. Its back paws bicycled as it hung down from Nick's hands.

"It's supposed to be mine," I said.

"I was just getting him out for you," said Nick. Nick handed me the cat. It was only a little bit bigger than my two hands put together. It wiggled around as if it wanted to get free. I didn't know what to do with it.

"He was the cutest one in the litter," said Barney. "I've been keeping my eye on him for you since he was born. He's friendly and loves to jump and he's full of curiosity. He reminded me of you."

I looked down at the kitten. It had green eyes and it squinched its eyes up at me as if maybe it didn't like me.

"Honey, aren't you going to thank Barney?" Mom asked.

I didn't know what to say. I really didn't want this kitten. Barking Barney didn't have any right just to give me any old animal he wanted.

"I don't know how to take care of a cat," I said.

"It's easier than a tadpole," said Barney. "He cleans himself. He's already trained to use the litter box."

I could tell Barney was going to go on and on, giving me a sales pitch about this cat. I couldn't take it anymore.

"I don't *want* him!" I shouted, close to tears.

Barney and Mom both looked hurt. The Pinecones looked at me as if I had just said the worse thing in the world. But didn't I have to be honest? I didn't want any of Barking Barney's pets. I wanted him out of my life. Yet, by turning down his kitten, I felt like such a meanie.

Barney coughed uneasily. "Well, naturally, Jodi, if you don't want the kitten, we can take him back. That's the advantage of knowing the owner."

Barney held his hands out to take the kitten back. I tried to put him in Barney's hands, but the kitten dug his claws into my forearm. I had to pry him loose, and then as soon as I let go of the kitten I felt awful.

The Pinecones were all looking at me as

if I were a murderer or something.

"Excuse me," I said. "I've got to go to my room." I ran upstairs. I didn't want the Pinecones around to see me in such a mess. I didn't want anybody around. And most of all, I didn't want one of Barking Barney's stupid kittens as a pet.

Look Up Sarcastic

I slammed the door to my room and sank down on my low beam. I wished the Pinecones hadn't happened to come over on this morning of all mornings. I watched LaToya swim up to the top of her aquarium. I should have been born a frog, an animal with a pea brain, separated from my mother at birth. I should have been born a real pinecone. Trees don't have mothers who remarry.

There was a knock at my door. "Go away," I said.

The door opened, as I knew it would. Darlene stuck her head inside. "Jodi, you okay?" she asked.

"Didn't you hear me say 'go away'?" I asked.

Darlene didn't answer my question. She sat down on the beam next to me.

"I think you and the other Pinecones had better go home," I said. "So much for your little plan to make sure that I got up on the right side of the bed. I guess it doesn't seem very cute now."

"We never meant it to be cute," said Darlene. "We thought it might cheer you up. Nobody blames you for being upset."

"I'm sick of hearing that nobody blames me. I'm not upset," I said. "It's just that Barney doesn't have any right to keep pawning off these silly pets on me."

"I thought the kitten was adorable," said Darlene. "Ti An is asking Barney if she can get one just like him."

"I'm so glad I've been able to drum up business for Barking Barney," I said sarcastically.

"Will you quit the sarcasm?" said Darlene. "I'm getting tired of it. You're driving yourself and everybody crazy because you're upset about your mom getting married."

"I'm *not* upset about Mom getting married. I've got other things that upset me. I just didn't want the stupid kitten. I can hardly take care of LaToya. Barney's got to learn he can't just unload every pet he can't sell on me."

"I don't think that's what he was doing," said Darlene. "I believed him when he said that he picked out the kitten especially for you."

"And you probably still believe in the Tooth Fairy and that one of us Pinecones is going to end up in the Olympics."

"It could happen," said Darlene.

"Give me a break," I said.

"I'm going to break your head if you don't stop being sarcastic all the time," threatened Darlene. "What's wrong with believing that one of us could be in the Olympics?"

"My dad's trained Olympians," I said. "Believe me, they are a different breed from us Pinecones. Patrick wouldn't know the first thing to do with somebody of Olympic caliber."

"Great," said Darlene. "Now you're putting down Patrick."

"What's the matter? Can't you take the truth?" I asked. "I'm just being honest."

"You know who says that all the time, don't you?" said Darlene. "Your friend Becky."

"Well, at least Becky isn't a loser like the rest of us," I said.

Darlene stood up. "Jodi Sutton, take that back."

"Take what back? I included myself. It's not like I called you losers and me a winner. Let's face it—we're all losers."

"*You're* the one who's losing," said Darlene. Darlene is captain of the Pinecones. She probably thought it was her job to straighten me out, but she didn't know what she was talking about.

I shrugged. "Look," I said. "So we're losers. Losing is supposed to be character-building. Nobody can say that the Pinecones aren't characters."

"This isn't a joke," said Darlene.

"I think it is," I said.

"Well, you'd better think again," warned Darlene. "You keep this up, and you'll be a real loser. You'll lose the best friends you ever had."

"I'll always have LaToya," I joked.

Darlene shook her head. "Okay, Jodi, you win. I'll get out of here. I can't talk to you when you're like this."

"Like what?" I asked, but I knew what Darlene was talking about. I was out of control. I was saying mean things to my friends, and I couldn't shut up my motor mouth.

Just then there was another knock on the door. The other Pinecones filed in. "I think we'd better go," said Darlene. "Jodi wants to be alone."

"You sure, Jodi?" asked Lauren. She sounded worried.

I sighed. "I'm sure." I wondered if Darlene would tell them that I had said we were all losers.

The Pinecones started to leave. "See you Monday, Jodi," Lauren called out.

"Yeah, things always look better at the gym," said Cindi. I knew she was just trying to be hopeful.

Darlene was the last one to leave. "Jodi, do me a favor. Look up the word 'sarcastic' in the dictionary."

I stared at her. That was the last thing I expected Darlene to say.

"What are you talking about?" I asked.

"I once had to look up 'sarcasm' for a paper I was writing," said Darlene. "Just do it. See where the word comes from—it comes from a Greek word."

"Is this some kind of test?"

"No," said Darlene. "It's just something I want you to do. You don't have to do it."

Darlene closed the door behind her. I think if she had told me I *had* to do it, I wouldn't have. I went to my desk and looked up the word 'sarcastic': *contemptuous and taunting language— biting gibes or cutting rebukes*, the dictionary said. It comes from the Greek word meaning *"to tear flesh, to bite the lips in rage."*

I was aware that my door was opening. I was so relieved. I was sure that it was Darlene again. Now I'd be able to apologize and make everything okay.

A tiny paw felt its way through the narrow opening. It was the kitten.

I picked it up. Its fur felt so soft. It licked my hand, its little tongue surprisingly rough, like a piece of sandpaper.

Then there was a knock at the door. But it wasn't Darlene. Mom stuck her head inside my room. "Jodi?" she asked.

She walked into my room. "Oh, good, the kitten is here. It got away from us." Mom sat down next to me and patted the kitten on the head. "Are you okay, Jodi? You know Barney was just trying to please you. He thought, with all the changes going on, you would want something that was yours alone."

"You never wanted me to have a cat before," I said.

"Well, your dad was allergic, and then when we moved here it just never occurred to me. But if you don't want the kitten, Barney will take him back to the store."

The kitten made a sound like a toy engine. "It's purring, I think."

"I think so, too," said Mom.

"Can I keep it on trial basis and see if I like it?" I asked her.

"You'll have to ask Barney," said Mom. She grinned. "But I'm sure he'll say that's one of the advantages of marrying into a pet store dynasty."

I tried to smile.

"By the way," she said. "The Pinecones all

seemed to leave in a hurry. Was anything wrong?"

I put my face down right next to the kitten. "No," I lied as I muttered into the kitten's fur.

I thought about the definition of sarcastic: To tear flesh, to bite one's lips in rage. Pretty dramatic language for something that seemed to just come off my lips without thinking. It sounded like someone out of control.

"What do you think?" I asked the kitten.

"What are you going to call him?" Mom asked me.

"I haven't decided whether I'm going to keep him," I reminded her.

"Well, even for a few days, shouldn't we give him a name?"

"I'm going to call him Sar-Cat."

"Sar-Cat?" asked Mom. "What language is that?"

"Greek," I said. "It's short for sar-*cat*-stic," I said.

"I don't get it," said Mom.

"I know," I said.

10

Motor Mouth

Darlene was cool to me when I walked into practice on Monday afternoon. I tried to pretend that nothing had happened. Darlene was wearing one of her bright pink leotards. "You look pretty," I said. Cindi and Lauren were being much quieter than usual. Everybody said hello to me, and no one mentioned the things that I had said on Saturday.

"Thank you very much," said Darlene politely, but her words were clipped.

"I think that I got up on the *right* side of the bed this morning," I said, trying to make a joke.

"That's good," said Darlene. "And to think, we weren't even there to check."

I laughed, grateful that Darlene had loosened

up enough even to make a little joke. Maybe things would change back, and we could all be comfortable and friends again.

"Hey, guess what?" I said. "I'm keeping the kitten for a few days."

"Oh," said Darlene. "You mean until you decide whether or not it's a loser?"

I swallowed hard. "I named it 'Sar-Cat' because it's short for 'sar-*cat*-stic.' "

"That's a sorry name for a cat," said Lauren. "I think you could have named it something cuter, like Tigger, in *Winnie the Pooh*."

"Or Hobbes," said Ti An. "I think the kitten is going to grow up to look like the tiger in the *Calvin and Hobbes* comic strip."

"Obviously Jodi likes a sar-*cat*-stic name," said Darlene, and I could tell that she hadn't forgiven me.

We went out onto the gym floor, and I couldn't help wondering if maybe I had finally done it. The Pinecones and I weren't friends anymore.

The gym looked dingier to me than it ever had before. It's in a cement-block warehouse, and Patrick has put all his money into equipment for us and very little into prettying the gym up. There are no skylights, just high windows around the ceiling and bright fluorescent lights. The whole place still looked like a warehouse. I couldn't imagine it as a setting for a wedding.

Mom and Dad had got married in a beautiful church. I've seen the pictures. Dad wore a tuxedo. Mom and Dad look so young in the pictures. Mom was only nineteen when she got married. She and Dad were still competing in gymnastics. Their best man went on to compete in the Olympics the next year.

Mom was almost the same age then as my sister Jennifer is now. I can't even imagine Jennifer getting married. I wonder if Mom and Dad had been older whether they would have stayed married. Mom says that she thinks that Dad and she fell in love with the *idea* of being married. Everyone thought they were a wonderful couple because they were both great gymnasts. "But our personalities were so different," says Mom. "All we really had in common was gymnastics."

Dad doesn't talk about it much, but he probably agrees. He's remarried now to Melissa, a woman who works in a bank. I don't really know her very well. When I visit, she's very nice to me, but we don't laugh and talk much, not the way I do with Mom.

Mostly Dad wants to talk to me about gymnastics. I think he's disappointed that I'm not Olympic caliber. Jennifer's too old for serious competition now, and she's committed to becoming a pilot or an astronaut. She doesn't want to compete seriously anymore. She says it takes too much time.

Everybody, even my dad, has always assumed that I don't have the talent or discipline to be a real champion. Mom says that she's glad I have Patrick as a coach, because Patrick doesn't push me further than I can go. Mom says that the reason I fit in so well with the Pinecones is because they are such nice, normal kids, not super-athletes. "The Pinecones are a team that care about one another," says Mom. "They always band together."

I looked around at my little band. We were a bunch of intermediates without much ambition. The Atomic Amazons and other teams can usually beat us with ease. Maybe the only thing that held us together was the fact that we were losers, just like the only thing that held Mom and Dad together was the fact that they were winners, at least for a while. It was a depressing thought.

"Jodi," said Patrick, "you're sleepwalking through your warm-ups. Put a little oomph into it."

"That's not a word that Jodi likes," Lauren reminded Patrick. "She doesn't think it's technical enough."

"I think Jodi knows that I mean," said Patrick.

"I want you to look awake. We're going to be working on the back flips again today."

"I want to work on the vault," I said. It seemed to me that we hadn't worked on the vault in a long time.

"You usually hate the vault," Cindi reminded me.

"It's my worst event, but that just means I need the most practice in it," I said. "I think that's what I should work on the most."

"That's a good attitude, Jodi," said Patrick, "but today we're going to work on back flips." He smiled at me. "Let's perfect your standing back flips, and then we'll let you put a string of them together."

I put my hands on my hips. I really didn't need to practice back flips. I needed practice on the vault.

"I do back flips just fine," I said. "You know I need work on the beam."

"Jodi," Patrick said in a warning voice, "I'm the coach around here. We'll schedule beam time for you later. Right now, I want all the Pinecones to work on their floor routines, and we're going to continue to work on our back flips."

"We should be learning double backs," I argued. "Are we going to be stuck doing stupid back flips forever?" I knew as soon as the words were out of my mouth that I was going too far.

"Stupid" seemed to be the only word I could say lately. Once again it was old motor mouth in control, not me.

Patrick looked at me. "Less back talk please and more back flips. I seem to have to repeat that to you a lot lately."

"Right," I muttered, "just because you're happy to have the Pinecones stay mediocre forever."

"Jodi!" said Patrick sharply. "That's enough."

"Sorry," I mumbled.

"You owe an apology not just to me but to all the Pinecones," he said. I could tell that Patrick was really angry.

"Don't worry about us," said Darlene. "We're getting used to Jodi calling us losers."

Patrick put down his clipboard. "Jodi," he said, "go to my office. I want you to stay there and think things through. I'll be up to talk to you as soon as I can."

"I . . . I . . . " I stammered, "I don't want to go to your office. I want to practice my back flips."

"Until you can control your back talk, I'm not interested in your back flips," said Patrick. He pointed to his office. I didn't have a choice. I had to go. I had come into gymnastics determined that today would be different, that I wouldn't be in a lousy mood. But nothing had changed. Maybe it was the place that was wrong, not me.

11

Patrick Calls
My Bluff

Patrick's office is a tiny room. One wall has a crammed bookshelf full of books on gymnastics. There are a few Olympic posters taped to the wall. My dad's got his posters framed, and he has photographs. One of them is signed by Nadia Comaneci, the great Rumanian Olympic gymnast.

I waited nervously for Patrick to come, but he took a long time. I realized that I must have really made him angry. Every once in a while Patrick sends one or the other of us out of the gym to cool off if we're having a temper tantrum. It's happened to all of us Pinecones at one time or another, but I couldn't remember his ever making one of us wait alone for so long.

I tried to pace around the little office, but there really wasn't any room to move.

Finally I decided I had had enough. I was going back down to the gym. There really wasn't anything that Patrick could do to me. It wasn't as if he had any real authority over me. I'd just tell him that I had gotten bored and that I had to get out, for my own sanity.

I was halfway down the hall when I heard Patrick's footsteps on the metal steps that lead from the gym to the second floor.

Patrick saw me outside the office. "Where are you going?" he asked. His voice sounded friendly and concerned. It wasn't threatening, and yet I felt as if he were accusing me.

"I got tired of waiting," I said defiantly. My own voice was a little shrill and even squeaky.

"I wanted to give you a chance to be alone for a while," said Patrick. He guided me back into his office and sat behind his desk.

I stood shifting my weight to my right foot. I put my right hand on my hip. I wanted Patrick to know that I didn't think there was anything we needed to talk about.

"Sit down, Jodi," said Patrick easily.

"I've been sitting up here with nothing to do for half an hour," I complained. "I should have been doing gymnastics."

"You would have been doing gymnastics if you

had been able to act as part of a team, but lately that's not been true," said Patrick. "I figured we needed to talk."

I slumped down in a chair. "I guess this is the time for one of our little 'talks' with Patrick — where you make everything all right."

He frowned at me. "Jodi, sarcasm isn't what I expect from you. It's not your style."

"A lot you know about me," I said. "I even have a sarcastic cat."

"I do know you," said Patrick. "And you'd be the last person I'd think of as being sarcastic. It's usually weak kids who have to be sarcastic. It's a tool for bullies."

I thought about Becky and how she always had a sarcastic crack for everyone and how her cracks hurt. Becky might be a bully, but she wasn't weak.

I bit my lip.

"Jodi, I can't help you if you won't tell me what's wrong. But you and I both know that you haven't been yourself these past few weeks. I've got a feeling that you're more upset about your mom's wedding than you even know. It's perfectly human."

"Oh, give me a break," I protested. "Everybody's trying that line on me, and I think it's just a bunch of hooey."

"Then what do you think is bothering you —

because I'm telling you, Jodi, you haven't been yourself."

Something inside of me just snapped. I was so sick of people telling me I wasn't being myself. Why did everybody think something was wrong with me?

"Did it ever occur to you that something might be wrong with the way you coach us?" I demanded.

Patrick drew back his head as if I had just slapped him, but I couldn't stop myself. "Yeah, our whole gym is just for losers. There's got to be a reason why we lose all the time."

"Exactly what do you think that reason is?" Patrick asked me. His voice was quiet, but I could tell he was angry.

"Uh . . . well," I started to stammer.

"Yes?" he asked.

I took a deep breath. I had to say what I felt, didn't I? I thought that Patrick was a lousy coach. He was the reason why we lost all the time.

"My dad is a great coach," I said. "And he runs the gym like a military academy. Everything is very precise, and you know weeks in advance exactly what you're going to be doing."

"Jodi, I want my gymnasts to have *inner* discipline. I don't believe it's something that can be imposed on you."

"Well, maybe inner discipline is a myth . . .

and we need something much more — like my dad's way of doing things."

"When you started here, Jodi, you and your mother both said that you were looking for a slightly looser structure. I understood that you hadn't thrived in your mom and dad's gym. Until the past few weeks, I've been pleased with your progress. You were an important and popular part of your team. I thought you were enjoying yourself and learning. That's all I ask of my students."

"That's not enough," I snapped.

"It's *you* who aren't giving enough," said Patrick. "Jodi, I know this is a tough time for you, but you've got to stop blaming all of us around you. If you won't face the fact that you're upset, I can't help you."

"I know what's upsetting me," I said. "I don't like the loosey-goosey atmosphere of the gym. Maybe you aren't the right coach for me."

My words just hung in the air. I wanted to take them back, swallow them up again. Patrick knew me well enough to know that I didn't mean them. He'd talk me out of it.

Patrick didn't say anything for the longest time. I finally had to ask him what he was thinking.

Patrick sighed. "Jodi, I can't make that decision for you."

"What decision?" I cried.

"I can't persuade you that I'm the right coach for you. That's a gut decision. I've always felt that you and I worked well together. I've admired your energy and spirit. However, I'm not the perfect coach for everybody. That's something that you and your mom will have to decide."

I stared at him. Patrick had called my bluff. I didn't want to quit the Pinecones and leave Patrick. Those words had just flown out of my mouth because I wanted to hurt somebody, and Patrick had been in the way.

12

Cry Wolf

I knew the Pinecones would be waiting for me in the locker room to find out what had happened to me during my talk with Patrick. It was almost a ritual with us Pinecones; whenever Patrick called one or the other of us on the carpet, the others waited.

"Us Pinecones." I hadn't used the words in a long time. Patrick had said that it was my choice if I wanted to remain a Pinecone. I couldn't imagine what my life in Denver would be like without the Pinecones.

I thought about not going into the locker room at all. I could just go sit in Mom's car and wait for her. But I wanted to talk to Mom even less than I wanted to talk to the Pinecones.

I opened the door to the locker room. I could hear Ashley's high, pip-squeaky voice. "I bet Patrick really gave it to Jodi. She's been impossible lately."

"Patrick wouldn't yell at her," said Lauren. "And Jodi's got a lot on her mind."

"I bet Patrick straightened her out," said Darlene. "Jodi just needs someone like Patrick to talk to."

Everyone was so used to Patrick being able to solve all our problems. But he hadn't been able to solve mine.

I shoved the door further open so that everybody could see I was there. Lauren's gym bag was perched in front of my locker. It didn't bother me.

"Are you okay?" Lauren asked.

"Did Patrick yell at you?" Ti An asked.

"He didn't yell," I said. "He just said that maybe he wasn't the right coach for me."

"Very funny, Jodi," said Darlene. "I think you've taken this sar-*cat*-stic thing way too far. It's time to give it a rest. We're sick of it."

"I'm not kidding, Darlene," I said. "That's what he said."

"Oh, sure," said Cindi. "Patrick told you to get another coach. Darlene's right. You've got to stop jerking us around like this. We've been patient. We know you're going through a hard time, but be honest with us. You were always honest."

I felt like the little shepherd in the fairy tale who cries wolf just to scare his family and friends. Finally a wolf really does come, and nobody believes him. I couldn't remember whether the little shepherd boy gets eaten or not.

"I *am* being honest." My teammates stared at me as if it were dawning on them that I might be telling the truth.

"I don't believe you," said Darlene flatly. She put on her jacket. The other Pinecones were already dressed. Darlene and the others kept darting funny looks at me, as if they thought I had suddenly contracted a contagious disease.

"Do you want us to wait for you?" asked Darlene.

"Don't bother," I said.

I noticed Darlene and Cindi whispering together as they left the locker room. Lauren gave me a worried look as she left. "Are you sure you don't want us to wait?" she asked.

"Forget it," I mumbled.

I was left alone in the locker room. I didn't cry. I'm not a crybaby. I slammed my locker shut. I threw on my clothes. I didn't bother to comb my hair.

I pushed open the door to the locker room. Jared was waiting outside the locker room.

"Cindi's not here," I told him.

"I know," said Jared. "She and all the Pinecones are upstairs talking to Patrick. They said it was something very important. " Jared stared at me. "How come you're not with them?"

"Because I'm *not* a Pinecone," I muttered under my breath.

"Is something wrong, Jodi?" Jared asked.

I took the stairs to Patrick's office two at a time. I was sure that everybody was talking about me behind my back. I stopped just outside the open door to Patrick's office. I pressed my back against the wall.

"Jodi's trying to scare us," I heard Darlene say. "She said you said that you weren't the right coach for her — that maybe she should quit the Pinecones. We know you didn't say that."

"This is between Jodi and myself," said Patrick.

"It isn't!" cried Cindi. "You can't just let Jodi quit the team. If she's planning on doing that we have a right to know."

"Girls, you have to consider that it might be possible that Jodi might be better off in another gym. I'm not the perfect match for every gymnast. Maybe Jodi finds working out in the same gym where her mother works claustrophobic."

"She never complained until a couple of weeks ago," said Lauren. "Patrick, you've got to talk her out of leaving. This is stupid."

"If Jodi's really unhappy, she has to make her own decision," said Patrick.

"At least talk her into staying until her mom's wedding," argued Darlene. "I don't think Jodi should make any decision until her mom's wedding."

I stood there out in the hall, feeling creepier than I had ever felt in my life. I'm not the type to eavesdrop. It's just not like me. I've got a lot of faults, but being sneaky isn't one of them.

I took a step inside. "Why does everybody keep thinking that Mom's wedding is the problem?"

"Jodi!" shouted Darlene. "How long have you been standing there?"

"Long enough to hear you all talking about me," I admitted.

Patrick twirled a pencil in his hand. "I'm sorry, Jodi. Your teammates were just very upset."

"Yeah, I heard," I said through gritted teeth.

"They were upset because they care," Patrick reminded me.

I bit my lower lip. I knew that he was telling me the truth, but it didn't make it any easier to hear.

"I don't care what Patrick says," said Cindi. "You've just got to put off making any decision until after your mom's wedding. Don't you think so, Patrick?"

"I think that Jodi should talk to her mom," he said.

"You all keep telling me that this is about Mom's wedding, but it's not," I insisted.

"It's a proven fact that a million ants can't be wrong," said Lauren.

"What does that mean?" I asked.

"Well, if a million ants show up at a place where you're having a picnic, it proves that it's a good place to have a picnic."

"That doesn't make any sense."

"Since when do Pinecones have to make sense?" asked Cindi.

"Does anyone remember the story about the boy who cried wolf?" I asked.

"Sure," said Darlene.

"What happens? Does he get eaten? I can't remember."

"I think he learns not to cry wolf when there's no wolf," said Darlene. "Isn't that how most fairy tales end?"

"I think he gets eaten," teased Lauren.

We weren't making any sense. I didn't know if I could ever get along with teammates who tried to make sense all the time.

Patrick listened to us, but he didn't say anything. I wondered if he was mad at me.

"Patrick," I asked, "is it all right if I take Darlene's advice and wait until the wedding to make up my mind?"

"I think that would be a very good idea," said Patrick. "But don't wait too long to talk to your mom about what you're feeling."

I started to protest that they were all wrong again, that my feelings had nothing to do with Mom and the wedding. But I didn't get the words out. For once, my motor mouth seemed to have run out of gas.

13

Only Human

Mom drove me home. I found myself tongue-tied. I thought I was just going to spill my guts, let everything out, but instead I couldn't say a word.

Mom was chattering on and on about how excited she was because she had found a dress-maker who wasn't very expensive. Mom was going to have a beautiful pale-ivory-colored suit made.

"But I'm most excited about the idea she came up with for you and Jennifer. Remember I said that I wanted it to be informal? I didn't want my two beautiful girls in a stuffy typical bridesmaid dress. The dressmaker knows that we're all gymnasts. She's making a beautiful black-and-white dress with these adorable polka-dot bicycle pants underneath and a kind of pouf in the back. It's very modern."

"Polka-dot bicycle pants!" I exclaimed. "We'll look like we belong in a circus."

"No, you won't. I promise you. Trust me," said Mom.

I sighed when she said the words: "Trust me."

"What's wrong, honey?" Mom asked. "I think you'll love the dress."

"It's not the dress that's bothering me!" I snapped. I hadn't meant to snap, but words came out of me these days with a tone of voice that I didn't intend.

I could tell that Mom wanted me to be excited about the dress, but couldn't she at least see that something was wrong with me? Besides, in black-and-white polka dots, Jennifer and I would probably end up looking like dominoes.

We pulled into the driveway. I opened the door almost before Mom had put on the brakes.

"Jodi, hold your horses," said Mom. I jumped out of the car as if I were jumping out of my skin. I couldn't wait to get up into my own room.

I flung open the front door. I forgot about Sar-Cat. He must have heard the car and been waiting for us. He bounded out the front door and into the driveway.

"Mom, Sar-Cat got out!" I yelled.

My yelling startled Sar-Cat. He darted out into the street, just as a car was coming.

I sprinted down the front steps after him. I heard brakes screech.

"Jodi!" screamed Mom.

The car grazed my calf as it stopped.

"Crazy kid!" shouted the driver at me. I didn't care. I ran to the other side of the street. Sar-Cat stopped on the far side of the street. His tail twitched back and forth, but he didn't move. It was as if I had scared him by almost getting killed.

"Please, Sar-Cat, don't move . . . don't run away." I crouched down so I would be on Sar-Cat's level. Sar-Cat's tail continued to twitch back and forth.

Mom came up behind me. "Jodi, you could have gotten killed!"

"Shh," I warned her. I held out my hand to Sar-Cat. Slowly he walked toward me. When he got within a foot, I grabbed him. I held him close.

"I was so sure that he'd run away. He doesn't know us very well," I said.

"Jodi, Jodi," said Mom, "you scared me half to death. You know you shouldn't have run out into the street like that."

"I couldn't let Sar-Cat run away." I was crying.

I guess the car almost hitting me had scared me more than I realized. Mom put her arm around me.

"Let's go inside," she said.

I couldn't stop crying. Mom guided me into the house.

We collapsed together on the living room couch. I still had Sar-Cat in my arms.

"Jodi, I've been so worried about you," said Mom. "I knew you were upset about the wedding, but I thought you'd come around. It's only human to be upset, but — "

"I didn't know you were worried about me," I said.

"I should have said something earlier. I thought you just needed time to get used to the idea. I wanted to give you some space. Maybe I gave you too much space."

"I didn't want Sar-Cat to get killed, and I don't really want to leave the Pinecones," I blurted out.

"Leave the Pinecones!" exclaimed Mom. "What are you talking about? You can't be serious."

I nodded. "You've been so busy thinking about the wedding all the time, you didn't even know I was thinking of quitting the Pinecones," I accused her.

"But, Jodi, you don't want to leave the Pinecones. That doesn't make sense."

"The Pinecones never make sense," I sniffed.

"I don't think that's true," said Mom. "I think the Pinecones have always made sense for you. I think it's you and me who haven't made much sense lately. The poor Pinecones have been your whipping boy."

I petted Sar-Cat's head. "Are you saying that I'm a horrible person 'cause I've been treating the Pinecones like I'm Becky?"

"Jodi, you'll never be Becky. I think maybe I let things get a little bit out of control myself. I knew you were upset, but maybe it was easier on me to let you get mad at the Pinecones."

"You were the one who told me that the Pinecones care about each other. I've been mean to everybody."

"Think of all the times that you've been there for the Pinecones. When Cindi broke her leg and wanted to quit, you helped talk her out of it. When Lauren was so tied up in knots about her mom running for mayor, you were the one who helped her. You've done your share for the Pinecones. They aren't ready to quit on you."

"I know . . . I think they expected Patrick to be able to make everything okay, but he only said that I had to make up my own mind, and I should talk to you."

"Patrick's a very smart man. There's a reason why he's my man of honor. Dad's not alive to give me away. I asked Patrick if he would give me away and told him he'd by my 'man of honor.' "

"Mom, that's so hokey. You're supposed to have a *maid* of honor. Besides, Patrick might not want to be your man of honor after the way I've been treating him lately."

I don't think it's Patrick you've been mad at," said Mom. "It's me . . . and *Dad*."

"Dad?" I exploded. "What does he have to do with this?"

"Jodi, I think you wanted to protect your dad. Even though he's remarried himself, my getting married means you have to give up any fantasies you've had of us getting back together."

"I don't have those fantasies," I said angrily. "That sounds like you got it out of a stupid book about what to say to your daughter when you get remarried."

"Every time you say 'stupid' lately, I know that you're really upset," said Mom. "I think getting mad at Patrick was a strange way of trying to stay loyal to your dad."

"I don't get it," I argued, but not as angrily as before. Some of what Mom was saying did make sense.

"Patrick and your dad are both coaches, and you couldn't face getting mad at me and Barney."

I sighed. "Did Patrick talk to you about me?" I asked.

Mom shook her head. "Patrick has always respected your privacy, but he did tell me that he thought you had more feelings about this wedding than you knew how to control. He wanted us to talk. I think I'm to blame, too. I wanted my own fantasy."

"What was your fantasy?" I asked.

"That you would instantly love Barney as much as I did, and that everything about this wedding would go smoothly and happily."

"It doesn't sound like a bad fantasy," I admitted to Mom.

"Sometimes reality is even better than fantasy. You know, there is something so easy and kind about Barney. He's got a heart as big as yours."

"So this wedding's your fantasy," I said.

"In a way," said Mom. "I'm marrying the man I love and trust, and I want you and Jennifer and Patrick standing up for me."

"Is Patrick wearing a dress with black polka dots?" I teased Mom.

"No," said Mom. "He says he doesn't look good in polka dots."

"Mom," I said seriously, "what if I hate it when you're married to Barney? What if I always hate having Nick the Pest around as a younger brother?"

"Jodi, why did you risk your life for a kitten that you said you didn't want?"

I looked down at Sar-Cat. "I don't know."

"I do," said Mom. "You're a girl with a huge heart. You've got room in it for your dad and for me and for Jennifer, and for a new cat. You've even taken good care of poor old LaToya up there. You'll find room in it for Barney and Nick. Maybe not right away. It'll take a long time for all of us. Nobody's expecting this to be easy. You're only human."

"I don't know why that's supposed to be so comforting," I complained.

"Maybe because it means that we all make mistakes and get mad at the wrong people some of the time," said Mom. "It's comforting to think that we all do it."

"I don't think I've been very comforting to the Pinecones," I said.

"The Pinecones are tough," said Mom. "They haven't given up on you."

"I haven't given up on them, either," I said.

"I know that," said Mom. "But you'd better let them know it. They're only human, too."

14

Not a Jerk
Forever

I went into the locker room determined, for the first time in a long time, to honestly have a good day. I'd straighten things out with Patrick and tell him that he was the coach for me. I'd tell my teammates that I was sorry I had been such a witch. Everything would turn out just fine. It's easy in your daydreams to think that just by saying a few words you can make everything right again. It's harder when you're face to face with the people you've been rotten to.

I knew I had to start with Darlene. She'd been the one who had tried to reach out to me and stuck by me.

I had it all planned out. I'd start by telling Darlene about my bridesmaid's dress. Darlene loves clothes so much, she'd know that I wanted to be friends again. Then when we were back talking comfortably again, I'd tell her that I was sorry for the way I had been acting. It would be too mushy to go in and apologize to Darlene right off.

So that was my plan. I forgot about Becky. I guess I had been acting so much like her that she hadn't been on my mind much lately. It was a mistake to ever forget about Becky.

Becky was changing into her leotard right next to Darlene. I ignored her and started talking to Darlene. "My mom's definitely settled on polka dots for my bridesmaid's dress. It's even got bicycle pants. I have to go try it on later this afternoon after practice. Will you go with me?"

"Uh . . . I don't know," stammered Darlene. "I might have something that I need to do."

"But I really want you there," I said.

Darlene looked confused and a little angry, and I knew right away that I had gone about it the wrong way. I should have apologized first. As far as Darlene knew, I was still the same kid who was calling her teammates losers and saying that Patrick wasn't a good coach.

"Polka-dot bicycle pants at a wedding!" exclaimed Becky. "I can't believe that! That's the worst taste I can imagine."

"Mom says it's a very sophisticated dress. It's got a black top," I said defensively.

"You'll look like a clown," shrieked Becky. "But then that's very appropriate. This whole wedding is a joke."

It was strange listening to somebody else being sarcastic. It really did sound whiny. "You're the one who's a joke," I said to Becky. "Mom says my dress is terrific, and I believe her."

"Your mom thinks having a wedding in a gym is good taste," said Becky. "Of course, she's marrying a guy whose *name* is a joke."

I grabbed Becky's arm and swung her around. "Barking Barney is not a joke. Take that back."

"I didn't say he is. I said his name is."

"He's a very nice man," I heard myself shouting at Becky. "He's got more niceness in his little finger than you have in your whole body."

Becky shrugged. "Well, it's kind of a fitting name for your new father. After all, the Pinecones already have a Big Beef in the family. Big Beef and Barking Barney, the four B's for the Pinecones. I don't know why everything you Pinecones do has to turn into a gag."

"You're the one who needs the gag," I said to Becky. "Don't you say anything against Darlene's dad or Barking Barney. They're both terrific men." I let go of Becky's arm and looked at the Pinecones. None of their eyes would meet mine.

I knew I had to fight Becky for all of us. "You're such a turkey," I said. "You just like to pick fights with the Pinecones because you have nothing better to do. Mean things just come out of you like hot air."

"Out of *me*?" protested Becky. "I hear *you're* the one who's thinking of leaving the Pinecones because you've finally realized they're terminal losers."

"Oh, Becky," I said, finally using my sarcasm for something constructive. "You're just jealous."

"Jealous?" exclaimed Becky. "Of the Pinecones?"

And that's when I realized that it was really true. Becky was sarcastic and mean to us all the the time because she was jealous. The Pinecones had something she could never have. Becky was physically strong, and I guess sometimes I get that confused with being a strong person. There are different kinds of weakness. Becky might be able to beat Darlene in a meet, but she couldn't hold a candle to her as a friend.

"Yeah," I said, "because the Pinecones always stick up for each other. You've got *nobody* to stick up for you."

Becky stuck her nose in the air and left the locker room in a huff. I think I had struck too close to the truth for her to hear.

"What a jerk!" said Lauren. "At least you won't

have to listen to Becky anymore if you leave Patrick's."

"I'm the one who's been the jerk."

"I'll second that," said Darlene.

"I meant what I said to Becky. I don't want to leave the Pinecones. You're the ones who've been there for me," I said. "You never gave up on me. Especially you, Darlene."

Darlene looked embarrassed.

"She kept telling us that you'd come around, that you were only upset about your mom's wedding."

"It's not that I'm not happy that Mom's happy," I said.

"Yeah, but you wished things could stay the way they were. I know all about that," said Cindi. "That's how I felt when Patrick first let boys in the gym."

"We figured sooner or later you'd come to your senses," said Darlene.

"It was later, wasn't it?" I said softly.

"You weren't exactly fun to be around," Darlene admitted.

"Yeah," said Lauren. "You were being a real pain in the butt, but I knew you wouldn't stay that way forever."

Suddenly I started to laugh. I realized that I hadn't laughed like that in weeks. It felt so good.

We all filed out of the locker room to get to practice. I stopped Darlene.

"I really owe you a special apology," I said. "You never gave up on me."

"The truth was that I missed you," said Darlene. "I hated having this mean impostor going around looking like Jodi but sounding like Becky."

"Was I that bad?" I asked.

"You came close," she said.

"Sorry," I said. "I can't believe how I took it out on you guys."

Darlene grinned at me. "Why do you think they write songs about 'you always hurt the ones you love'?" she asked.

"I guess I proved I love you all, then, didn't I?" I said.

Darlene nodded. "We knew it all the time," she said. "We also knew that you wouldn't stay a jerk forever."

Somehow those were the most comforting words I'd ever heard.

Made for Each Other

I put on my bridesmaid's dress. The velvet felt so soft around the top, and the polka-dot bicycle pants didn't look silly. They had beautiful black velvet drops against white satin.

"What do you think?" I asked Sar-Cat, who was sitting on the beam staring up at me — or up at LaToya. I think Sar-Cat had it in mind that LaToya would make a great meal someday.

Sar-Cat didn't answer me. He licked his paw.

"That must mean that you like the dress," I said to Sar-Cat.

I stepped out of my room and knocked on Mom's door. Sar-Cat followed me.

Jennifer was already with Mom, helping her

fix her hair. Jennifer and I had on identical dresses.

"You look beautiful," Jennifer and I said to each other right at the same time.

We started to giggle.

"You both look beautiful," said Mom.

"Not as gorgeous as you do," I said to Mom. Mom doesn't get dressed up very often. Her suit was made of a whispery soft material. In fact, I don't think I had ever seen her look so pretty.

She blushed. "I was the one who said I wanted to be informal at this wedding. Maybe I should have worn jeans."

"No," said Jennifer and I both at the same time again.

Mom laughed. "Are you two going to keep that up all day?" she asked.

"Right," I said. "When you say 'I do,' we're both going to say it along with you."

Mom smiled. "You know, this day wouldn't be half as happy for me if you two girls weren't by my side."

"I didn't make things easy for you," I admitted.

"So what else is new?" teased Jennifer. "Jodi never does things the easy way."

"This time I took being a pain in the neck to new heights," I confessed.

Jennifer did a double take. "You must have been pretty bad."

"I was out of control," I said.

"You were only human," said Mom.

"Funny," teased Jennifer. "I've never thought of Jodi as human." She gave me a fake punch on the arm.

Sar-Cat arched his back and hissed at Jennifer. Mom laughed. "Watch it," she warned. "Jodi's got a watch-cat guarding her now."

Jennifer bent down and scratched Sar-Cat on the head, showing him that she hadn't really meant to hurt me.

"Sar-Cat? What a strange name. What does it mean?"

"It's short for sar-cat-stic," I said.

"He was a present from Barney, wasn't he?" asked Jennifer. "He wanted to give *me* a pet, but I can't keep a cat in my dorm."

"You could have LaToya," I said quickly.

"Really?" asked Jennifer. "I think LaToya's cute. Are you sure you want to part with her?"

"If I keep her, she'll turn into cat food," I said. I didn't tell Jennifer that she'd have to clean LaToya's aquarium every week. There are some things that sisters have to find out for themselves.

Mom looked at her watch. "Girls," she sang, "I think it's time to get me to the gym on time."

Jennifer and I just groaned. "Does Barney know you sing in the mornings?" I asked.

"He likes it," said Mom.

"Maybe you two really were meant for each other," I admitted.

"We are," said Mom, giving me a hug, and I knew that she was truly happy. It was hard not to be happy for her.

16

A Toast to the Pinecones

We were crammed together — Mom, Jennifer, Patrick, Nick, and me — in the hallway outside of Patrick's office while the guests were arriving. Barney was downstairs with the minister. We were waiting for the wedding to start. The gym looked beautiful. Patrick had wound evergreen boughs and white flowers around the pillars and even around the bases of the uneven bars.

I had to admit that Nick the Pest looked adorable in a blue suit with a red bow tie. I told him he looked good.

"I'm scared I'm going to drop the ring," Nick admitted. "I wish Dad had let me glue it on the cushion."

"It won't fall off," I said. "Just pretend you're walking the balance beam."

"Boys don't do that," whined Nick. "Don't be stupid."

I sighed. "It's not going to be easy having you as a baby brother," I said.

"I'm not a baby," protested Nick.

I grinned at him. "You are to me."

"What are you grinning about?" Jennifer whispered to me.

"I just realized, I've always been the youngest. Now, finally, I've got somebody to pick on," I said.

"See? This wedding isn't all bad," said Jennifer. "I had trouble getting used to the idea. I was going off the wall there for a while."

"You, too?" I whispered. I always thought of Jennifer as so cool and collected.

"Yeah," said Jennifer. "But I guess the thing we've got to try to remember is that Mom's happy."

"Mom says that she doesn't expect us to love Barney and Nick right away," I said.

"I know," said Jennifer. "But I love the fact that Barney makes her happy."

I thought about Jennifer's words. "Me, too," I whispered.

Suddenly the strains of "Here Comes the Bride" drifted up from the gym.

"I like your choice of floor music," I whispered to Mom. She smiled nervously.

Nick put the ring on the cushion. He dropped

it. Jennifer had to help him find it on the floor.

"If he drops it during the ceremony, I'm going to belt him one," I said.

"Jodi," warned Mom, "I want a nonviolent wedding."

"I promise," I told her.

"You ready?" Jennifer whispered to me. We were supposed to walk down the aisle after Nick.

"Ready," I said.

"Are we really going to do what we planned?" Jennifer whispered to me.

"Mom said she wanted a loosey-goosey wedding," I whispered back.

Jennifer winked at me.

Patrick had a red carpet laid down the center of the gym. Everyone turned in their seats to look at me. Darlene looked beautiful in a red velvet dress with black ribbons. Cindi's bright red hair shone against a green dress that she was wearing. Lauren was dressed in purple. Ti An was wearing a yellow Vietnamese silk dress that her mother had made for her. Even Ashley looked pretty in blue. The Pinecones had gone all out for the wedding. They looked like a rainbow. I saw them smiling at me as Jennifer and I passed by. I smiled a little, but I was really nervous walking down the aisle with everybody watching me.

I don't think I had even seen Barney as we started down the aisle, but he was standing next to the minister. His eyes were incredibly warm as he smiled at Jennifer and me. I thought about Sar-Cat waiting for me at home and how Barney had said that he had picked him out so that I would have something of my very own in our new home.

Then I turned and watched Mom walk down the aisle with Patrick to meet her new husband.

The ceremony itself was very short. Nick didn't drop the ring, so my threat must have worked.

Mom and Barney kissed each other. They both looked so happy. All the guests burst into applause.

Then Mom and Barney turned and walked down the aisle.

"You ready?" Jennifer asked me.

I giggled.

"Take a deep breath," Jennifer said.

I breathed in deeply and then let it out. Jennifer's a much better gymnast than I am, but I had been practicing really hard.

We already had our backs to the guests. They expected us to turn and follow Mom and Barney down the aisle.

We didn't.

One after the other, we did back flips all the way down the aisle, flashing our polka-dot bicycle pants as we flipped. Everybody burst out laughing.

Mom and Barney had turned and were staring at us. Mom couldn't stop laughing.

She and Barney held their arms out and gave us both a big hug.

"You said you wanted loosey-goosey," I said to Mom.

"I did," said Mom. "Jodi, you made my wedding day so happy."

"I love you, Mom," I said.

"I love you, too, Jodi," said Mom.

Afterward all the guests got up. The adults got champagne. The kids got ginger ale with cherries in it. Everybody was milling around me, and I didn't get to the Pinecones for what seemed like ages. They were standing with Patrick. Finally I got through the crowd and joined them.

"That was a pretty good standing back flip," said Patrick.

"Did you like my control?" I teased him.

"Very much," said Patrick.

"I'm sorry for the way I acted before," I said. "I really think that you're the best coach in the whole wide world for me."

Patrick smiled at me. "I'm not sure about the whole wide world, but I do think we're a good match. Your dad's a good coach, too."

"I know," I said. "But I shouldn't have taken it out on you."

"I didn't want to lose you," said Patrick, "but

you had to make up your own mind."

"I did. Will you take me back?" I asked.

"It was never a question," said Patrick. "I like working with you, Jodi. You've got enthusiasm and spunk, and you keep me on my toes. I never know what you're going to do next."

"Is that a compliment?" I asked.

"You bet," said Patrick.

"Back flips at a wedding!" said Darlene, coming up to us, holding a champagne glass full of ginger ale. "That's one for the books."

"Becky would have said that it was in bad taste," Lauren said.

I looked around the room at Mom and Barney being toasted by all their friends.

"I've got a toast to make," I announced.

I raised my glass. "Here's to the Pinecones," I said. "They keep me sane, and they're the best team and the best friends that anybody could have."

I looked around at my friends and realized that I meant every word. Across the room, Mom raised her glass and toasted us all. I felt so giddy with excitement and happiness that I realized I was a little bit out of control. But it didn't matter. Being out of control sometimes is human, too.

About the Author

Elizabeth Levy decided that the only way she could write about gymnastics was to try it herself. Besides taking classes, she is involved with a group of young gymnasts near her home in New York City, and enjoys following their progress.

Elizabeth Levy's other Apple Paperbacks are *A Different Twist, The Computer That Said Steal Me*, and all the other books in THE GYMNASTS series.

She likes visiting schools to give talks and meet her readers. Kids love her presentation's opening. Why? "I start with a cartwheel!" says Levy. "At least I try to."